A Little Princess Story

I Don't Want to Go to the Hospital!

Tony Ross

Andersen Press USA

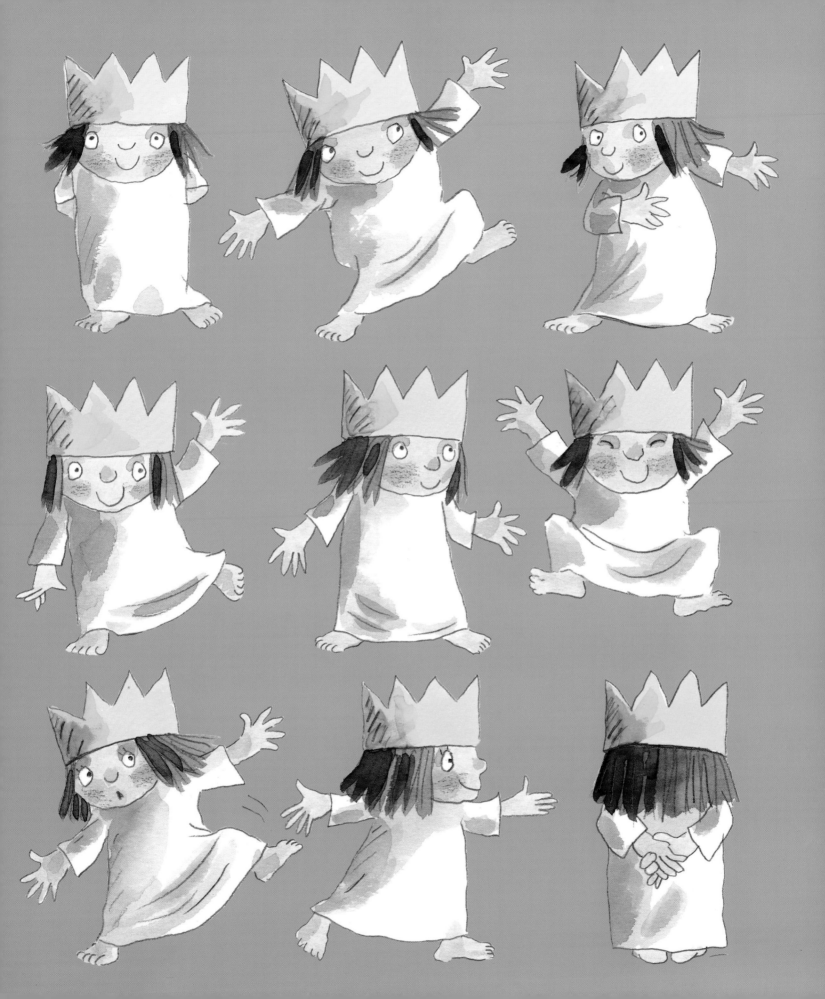

To Beth, who liked the hospital

American edition published in 2013 by Andersen Press USA,

an imprint of Andersen Press Ltd.

www.andersenpressusa.com

Paperback edition first published in 2010 by Andersen Press Ltd.

First published in Great Britain in 2000 by Andersen Press Ltd., 20 Vauxhall Bridge Road, London SW1V 2SA.

Published in Australia by Random House Australia Pty., Level 3, 100 Pacific Highway, North Sydney, NSW 2060.

Copyright © Tony Ross, 2000

Distributed in the United States and Canada by Lerner Publishing Group, Inc.

241 First Avenue North Minneapolis, MN 55401 U.S.A. www.lernerbooks.com

Color separated in Switzerland by Photolitho AG, Zürich.

Printed and bound in Malaysia by Tien Wah Press.

Library of Congress Cataloging-in-Publication Data Available.

ISBN: 978–1–4677–1155–5

1 – TWP – 8/3/12

"Ooo, Oww, Ooo," cried the Little Princess.
"My nose hurts!"

"You've got a little lump up there," said the Doctor.

"I'll get it out," said the General, drawing his sword.

"No," said the Doctor, "it won't come out.
Her Majesty must go to the hospital."

"No!" cried the Princess. "I don't want to go to the hospital!"

"It's nice at the hospital," said the Doctor. "You'll get candy and cards."
"I don't want to go," said the Princess.

"It's nice at the hospital," said the Queen, who had been there.
"I don't want to go," said the Princess.

"You'll meet lots of new friends in the hospital,"
said the Prime Minister.

"No! I don't WANT to go to the hospital!" said the Princess,
and she ran out of the room.

"Where is the Princess?" cried the Queen.
"It's time to go."

"She's not in her room," said the Maid.

"She's not in the trash can," said the Cook.

"She's not in any of my boats," said the Admiral.

"She's not on the roof," said the Gardener.

"She's in the attic!" said the King.
"I don't want to go to the hospital," said the Princess.

But the Little Princess had to go.

And the lump came out of her nose.

"Now that you are better," said the Queen,
"you can brush your teeth and comb your hair . . .

. . . and tidy your room and . . ."
"No!" cried the Princess . . .

"... I want my tonsils out!"

"But why?" said the Queen.
"I want to go back to the hospital," said the Little Princess.

"They treated me like a Princess in there."

Other Little Princess Books

I Want a Party!
I Want My Light On!
I Want My Mom!
I Want to Do It Myself!
I Want to Win!
I Want Two Birthdays!

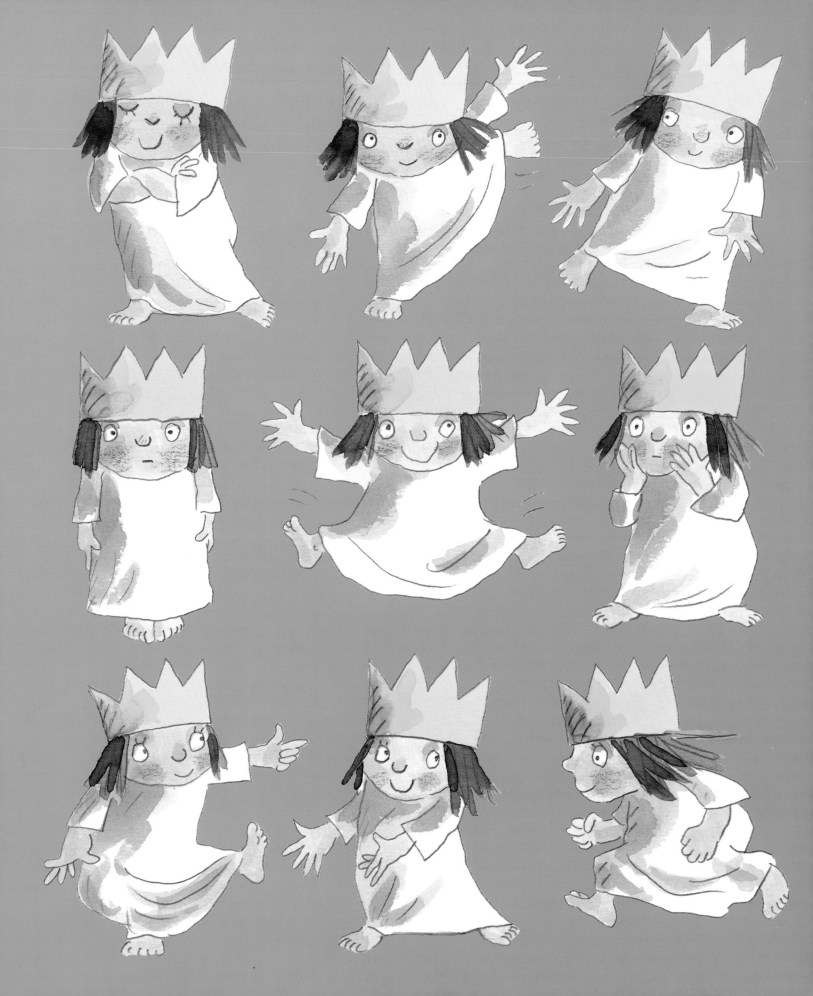